THIS BOOK BELONGS TO:

· ·

Written by Jan Astley, Gaby Goldsack and Kath Jewitt
The Night Before Christmas written by Clement C. Moore

Stories illustrated by Lesley Harker (Eunice McMullen),
Daniel Howarth (Advocate), Shelagh McNicholas, Claire Tindall
(Graham-Cameron Illustration) and Susan Winter (Eunice McMullen)
Additional art by Lisa Alderson (Advocate) and Jane Swift

This edition published by Parragon in 2010
Parragon
Queen Street House
4 Queen Street
Bath BA1 1HE, UK

ISBN 978-1-4075-7132-4

Printed in China

MAGICAL CHRISTMAS TALES

Bath New York Singapore Hong Kong Cologne Delhi Melbourne

CONTENTS

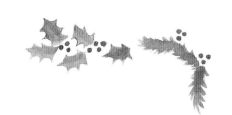

Mr Squirrel's Christmas

Mr Squirrel looked out the window of his woodland home and frowned. Although it was freezing outside, the woods were still full of animals laughing and smiling. Mr Squirrel huffed angrily to himself. He couldn't see what everyone had to be so happy about. And, to make matters worse, tomorrow was Christmas Day.

Mr Squirrel hated Christmas. As far as he was concerned, there was only one thing worse than Christmas Day itself, and that was all those silly animals pretending to be nice to each other just because it was Christmas. He really couldn't see what they all had to be jolly about.

"Stuff and nonsense," muttered Mr Squirrel, as he hammered a sign to his front door. "CHRISTMAS CANCELLED!" he read out loud. "There, that should stop everyone from bothering me for a while." And he went back inside to his cosy house.

CHRISTMAS CANCELLED!

Mr Squirrel didn't intend to go outside again until the festive season was well and truly over.

He was just sliding the bolts across the door, when – TAP, TAP – there was a knock on the other side. Mr Squirrel was furious. "Can't you read?" he shouted, as he swung open the door and glowered at whoever had dared to knock.

At first he couldn't see anyone. Then he looked down and saw a tiny dormouse standing on his doorstep. It was Dinky Dormouse, who lived next door. He had a big smile on his face and a colourful card in his hand.

"Merry Christmas, Mr Squirrel," he said shyly.

"GO AWAY," shouted Mr Squirrel.

"B...b...but I just wanted to give you this," stuttered Dinky Dormouse. He held out the colourful card for Mr Squirrel to take.

13

Mr Squirrel glanced at the card and shuddered. On it was a crowd of animals gathered around a brightly decorated Christmas tree singing carols.

"Can't you read?" he growled. "Christmas is cancelled as far as I'm concerned. Now buzz off!" And, with that, Mr Squirrel slammed the door in Dinky Dormouse's face.

You are invited to the Woodland Christmas Party. Starts 12 o'clock sharp in the glade. No need to bring anything but a smile.

He was just about to push the bolts across when something plopped onto his doormat. He couldn't believe his eyes. It was that horrible card. Mr Squirrel picked it up and read what it said inside.

"You are invited to the Woodland Christmas Party. Starts 12 o'clock sharp in the glade. No need to bring anything but a smile."

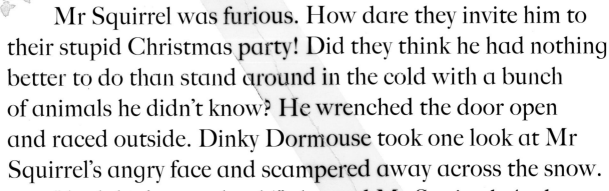

Mr Squirrel was furious. How dare they invite him to their stupid Christmas party! Did they think he had nothing better to do than stand around in the cold with a bunch of animals he didn't know? He wrenched the door open and raced outside. Dinky Dormouse took one look at Mr Squirrel's angry face and scampered away across the snow.

"And don't come back!" shouted Mr Squirrel. And just to make sure that he didn't, he chased after him. But he hadn't got far when – WHOOPS! – he tripped over a twisted tree root and landed with a thud on the ground.

"Are you all right?" asked Dinky Dormouse, helping him to his feet.

"Of course I am," snapped Mr Squirrel. He was about to stomp away when he gave a yelp. "Ouch!" He had twisted his ankle and could hardly walk.

"Let me help you," said Dinky. And although Mr Squirrel tried to wave him away, Dinky helped him back to his warm kitchen.

"Now, rest your foot on this stool," said Dinky, guiding him to his comfy chair beside the fire.

Mr Squirrel huffed and puffed, but it was no use – Dinky insisted on tending to his ankle.

"Now, doesn't that feel better?" said Dinky after he had wrapped Mr Squirrel's ankle in a clean bandage.

"I suppose it does," grunted Mr Squirrel reluctantly.

"Now I'll just make you a cup of acorn tea and I'll be on my way," said Dinky. And although Mr Squirrel tried to tell him to go away, Dinky got to work making him a lovely cup of tea.

As he busied himself in the kitchen, Dinky chattered away. Despite himself, Mr Squirrel sank back into his chair and listened. Dinky told him all about his family and woodland friends and the fun they always had together, especially on Christmas Day. He even sang Mr Squirrel one of the carols they enjoyed singing around the Christmas tree.

From time to time, Mr Squirrel found himself asking a question about who was related to whom, or who lived where. There was a lot that he didn't know about his neighbours. After a while, Mr Squirrel started to get an odd, fuzzy feeling inside. It wasn't a feeling he'd had before. Suddenly, he realized that he wasn't feeling grumpy. In fact, if he didn't know better, he'd think he was almost feeling happy.

By the time Dinky said it was time to go, Mr Squirrel didn't want him to leave. It was nice talking to somebody for a change.

After he had gone, Mr Squirrel wondered if perhaps he was lonely. Then he gave himself a good shake. Of course he wasn't lonely. After all, why would he want to waste his time babbling to a bunch of silly animals? That didn't get the acorns gathered or the dandelion wine brewed. But no matter what he told himself, he went to bed with a warm, fuzzy feeling in his tummy.

21

The next morning, Mr Squirrel awoke with
a tiny smile on his face. He felt so happy that he
decided to go outside and take down his silly sign.

As he tore it down, he saw something leaning
up against the frame of his door. It was a beautifully
carved walking stick, with an acorn for a handle.

Tied to it was a card saying, "Merry Christmas. Love from your woodland pals."

Mr Squirrel's face broke out into a big grin. It was the first Christmas present he had ever received. "It's just what I need," he said to himself. "How thoughtful."

Later, when he was counting his acorns, Mr Squirrel found himself humming an unfamiliar tune. "What is that?" he asked himself. Then he stopped humming as he remembered. It was the Christmas carol that Dinky had sung to him the previous evening. Mr Squirrel laughed at himself. He must be getting soppy in his old age.

Later that day, Mr Squirrel was dusting the mantelpiece when he saw something poking out from behind the mirror. It was the invitation to the Woodland Party. Dinky must have put it there before he left. Mr Squirrel pulled it out and read it thoughtfully to himself.

"You are invited to the Woodland Christmas Party. Starts 12 o'clock sharp in the glade. No need to bring anything but a smile."

Mr Squirrel drummed his claws on the card and thought hard. "It might actually be nice to spend Christmas Day with other animals."

He looked at the clock. It was five to twelve. If he was quick, he could just make it in time.

He limped to his pantry and loaded a basket up with acorns and dandelion wine.

Then he limped to a chest he kept hidden beneath his bed and dug out a sack of toys that he hadn't played with since he was a little squirrel. He had decided that he could take a smile to the party, and lots more besides.

As Mr Squirrel limped towards the glade, the smile on his face began to fade. What if he wasn't welcome at the party? After all, he was a grumpy old squirrel. He was always shouting at the other animals for making too much noise or getting in his way when he was out collecting acorns. He slowed down and was about to turn away when he heard somebody calling him. It was Dinky Dormouse.

"You came!" cried Dinky. "We hoped you would."
He rushed forwards and helped Mr Squirrel with his load.
"What do you have here?" laughed Dinky. "You didn't need
to bring anything. We just wanted you to come and enjoy
yourself."

"And so I will," said Mr Squirrel. "But I thought I'd bring
some food and drink, and toys for the children. It is Christmas,
after all. Oh, and thank you for my lovely present.
It's just what I need."

Before Mr Squirrel could take another step, a sea
of smiling faces surrounded him. Soon Mr Squirrel was
chattering away to all the animals as if he did it every day of
the week. Once he'd met everyone and even played a few games
of hunt the acorn, a small bunny came up to him and tugged at
his paw.

"'Scuse me, Mr Squirrel," squeaked the bunny. "But you're
not really grumpy, are you?"

Everyone gasped, and silence fell over the glade. Surely if anything was going to make Mr Squirrel angry, that was. But they needn't have worried. Mr Squirrel began to chuckle silently. Then he began to laugh out loud. Soon he was laughing so much that he had to hold his sides. One by one, everyone else joined in. Soon the woodland glade was filled with happy laughter.

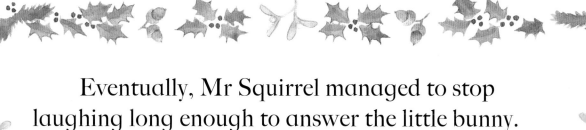

Eventually, Mr Squirrel managed to stop laughing long enough to answer the little bunny.

"No, I'm not grumpy," he smiled. "Not any more."

Later, after everyone had had their fill to eat and drink, Mr Squirrel handed out the toys to the children. As each one thanked him and planted a wet kiss on his cheek, he felt warm and fuzzy inside. Spending Christmas with others really was great fun.

"I just have one more thing to say," he said, raising a drink in his paw. "And that is – Merry Christmas, woodland friends!"

And from that day on, Mr Squirrel always shared Christmas with his woodland friends.

WE WISH YOU A MERRY CHRISTMAS

We wish you a merry Christmas!
We wish you a merry Christmas!
We wish you a merry Christmas
And a happy New Year.

Chorus
Glad tidings we bring
To you and your kin.
We wish you a merry Christmas
And a happy New Year!

Now bring us some figgy pudding,
Now bring us some figgy pudding,
Now bring us some figgy pudding,
So bring some out here.

(Repeat Chorus)

And we won't go until we've got some,
We won't go until we've got some,
We won't go until we've got some,
So bring some out here!

(Repeat Chorus)

LEAVE IT TO RUDOLPH

It was Christmas Eve in Lapland, and snowing hard. Santa and Mrs Claus were rushing around loading bulging sacks of presents onto Rudolph's sleigh. It was their busiest night of the year, and they were running late. It was also Rudolph's second year pulling the sleigh on his own, since he was the fastest.

"Hurry, hurry," urged Mrs Claus. "It's time for you to leave!"

"Just one more sack to go," answered Santa, huffing and puffing as he staggered towards the sleigh. But the ground was icy. Santa slipped and fell, landing with a **crash** in the snow.

"Ouch!" he cried. "I think I've twisted my ankle."

Mrs Claus helped Santa back into the house and found a bag of frozen peas to put on his swollen ankle.

"The cold will make it feel better," she explained.

Rudolph shook his head sadly. It didn't look as if Santa would be going anywhere in a hurry tonight. His ankle had puffed up like a balloon. He couldn't walk, much less climb up and down chimneys.

"What are we going to do?" wailed Mrs Claus. "Tomorrow is Christmas Day, and children everywhere must have their presents!"

"You'll have to go instead of me," sighed Santa, clutching his sore ankle.

"But I don't know where all the children live," replied Mrs Claus.

"Leave it to Rudolph," Santa reassured her. "He'll know what to do."

When Rudolph heard the plan he shook his head again. His memory wasn't very good, and he didn't have the other reindeer to count on. He wasn't sure he could remember where all the children lived. But Mrs Claus didn't want to disappoint the children, so she kissed Santa goodbye and climbed into the sleigh.

Things went well at first. Rudolph managed to remember where everyone lived, and he showed Mrs Claus where to go. But then they reached the very last town on their route – the town of Melford.

MELFORD

"Now, Rudolph," said Mrs Claus. "The first present I have to deliver here is a sparkly ballet dress for Sophie Smith. Do you know which house is hers?"

Rudolph looked around, feeling puzzled. He had forgotten where anyone lived in Melford.

Rudolph had to guess. He pointed a hoof towards a red door in a row of houses.

"23 Oldgrove Street?" asked Mrs Claus. Rudolph nodded, hoping for the best.

43

From then on, things seemed to go smoothly.

Rudolph helped Mrs Claus deliver a giant fluffy toy rabbit to Harry Bennett at 24 Oldgrove Street, and a shiny red bike to Emily Brown at number 25.

Last of all, Mrs Claus squeezed down the tiny chimney at 6 Walnut Lane to deliver a pair of silver and blue football boots to Samuel Jones. She even managed not to wake up the puppy that was asleep at the foot of the bed.

Then Mrs Claus and Rudolph headed back to Lapland, feeling very pleased with themselves.

When they got home, a relieved Rudolph went to his stable for a well-earned rest, and Mrs Claus went into the house to see Santa. His ankle was much better. "How did it go?" he asked.

"Rudolph remembered everything, even the children in the last town of all, Melford," said Mrs Claus proudly.

"Sophie at 23 Oldgrove Street got the ballet dress she asked for, and Harry at number 24 got his rabbit. We delivered the bike Emily wanted to number 25, and Samuel's football boots went to 6 Walnut Lane. Everything went very well."

As Santa listened carefully to what his wife was saying, his eyes grew wider and wider. Then he got up and pulled on his long, black boots.

"Wake up, Rudolph!" he called. "We're going out again."

"We have to go back to Melford," explained Santa to Mrs Claus. "Sophie Smith doesn't live at number 23 - that's where Samuel Jones lives. Sophie lives at 6 Walnut Lane. And Harry doesn't live at number 24 - that's Emily Brown's house."

Mrs Claus looked horrified. "Are you saying that everybody got the wrong presents?" she stuttered.

"That's exactly what I'm saying," nodded Santa. "Come on, Rudolph! We've got more work to do!"

When Santa and Rudolph got back to Melford, they could hear a cockerel crowing – it was Christmas morning! Santa shot in and out of chimneys as fast as he could, putting everything right. Luckily, his ankle had made a full recovery.

He quickly grabbed the toy rabbit from the end of Harry's bed and rushed over to Emily's house with it. He grabbed the shiny red bike from Emily's house and crept back to Harry's house with it.

Then Santa squeezed down the tiny chimney at 6 Walnut Lane and found the football boots that were meant for Samuel.

Sophie's puppy was at the foot of the bed, but he didn't stir. Santa wriggled back up the chimney and kept on sorting out the whole messy mix-up.

All that was left to deliver was the ballet dress to Sophie at 6 Walnut Lane. Santa squashed himself into the chimney one more time and placed Sophie's present on her bed next to the sleeping puppy.

"I'm not going back up that tiny chimney again," he thought. "I'm running out of time. I'll use the back door instead." But just as he was creeping out, Sophie's puppy ran into the back garden, barking loudly. He wanted to play with Rudolph!

"Ssssh," cried Santa. "You'll wake up the whole town." But the puppy didn't understand, and barked even louder.

"This time you CAN leave it to me," smiled Rudolph, who was standing patiently outside.

He lowered his head until he was touching noses with the noisy puppy. Then he said something to the puppy in animal language.

"Woof, woof, woof," replied the puppy, and he trotted back inside wagging his tail.

"Good job, Rudolph!" said Santa. "You may be a bit forgetful at times, but you've saved Christmas after all! Now let's go home!"

With one last weary effort, Rudolph leaped into the air. And by the time all the children woke up on Christmas Day, Santa, Rudolph, and the sleigh had completely disappeared. They were all back in Lapland with Mrs Claus...fast asleep!

Away in a Manger

Away in a manger, no crib for a bed,
The little Lord Jesus laid down his sweet head.
The stars in the bright sky looked down where he lay,
The little Lord Jesus asleep on the hay.

The cattle are lowing, the baby awakes,
But little Lord Jesus, no crying he makes.
I love you, Lord Jesus; look down from the sky,
And stay by my side until morning is nigh.

Be near me, Lord Jesus, I ask you to stay
Close by me forever, and love me, I pray.
Bless all the dear children in your tender care,
And take us to heaven, to live with you there.

A Very Special Gift

It was Christmas Eve, and Princess Rosie was very excited. She'd been saving for a long time, and now she had enough gold coins to buy her dad, the king, an absolutely fabulous present.

"I want something that's shiny and sparkly that costs lots and lots of money," she told the man behind the counter at the royal jewellers.

"How about this?" said the man, showing Princess Rosie a gold chain.

"Not expensive enough," said Princess Rosie.

"Then how about this?" he asked, holding out a shiny silver tie pin.

"Not sparkly enough," replied Princess Rosie.

"Well, how about this diamond ring?"

"Too small," declared Princess Rosie. "I want something much bigger and better than that to show my father just how much I love him."

As the man rummaged around desperately trying to find something suitable, Princess Rosie looked around the shop on her own. It was brimming with expensive things that sparkled and glowed. Surely there must be something her dad would like.

Suddenly, something big, shiny, and very, very expensive caught her eye. It was a beautiful clock.

Its face and hands were made of solid gold, and its numerals were formed from diamonds and emeralds. Princess Rosie had never seen such a fancy clock.

"I'll take that," she shouted, pointing an excited finger at the clock. "That really is a present fit for a king."

"But that's the most expensive thing in the shop," said the man. Then he gave an embarrassed cough. "Ahem, are you sure you can afford it, Princess?"

"Of course I can," laughed Rosie. Then she poured her gold coins out onto the counter.

"Er," gulped the man, "that looks like more than enough." He counted out the coins, then went to the till and took out a teeny-tiny little bronze coin. "Your change," he added, dropping it into Princess Rosie's hand.

Princess Rosie was so pleased with the clock that she couldn't wait for it to be delivered and decided to take it home straight away. "I just know Dad's going to love it," she thought as she raced back to the palace with her precious gift clutched in her arms.

Rosie was so busy thinking about how pleased her dad would be that she had spent so much money on him, that she didn't notice the icy puddle in the snowy courtyard.

"Ahhh," she screamed as she skidded and spun. "EEEEE," she cried as she lost control of her feet. "Oooooh," she gasped, as she fell on her bottom and the clock landed beside her with a CRASH!

Princess Rosie scrambled to her feet and rushed over to the clock. Perhaps she'd been lucky and it had landed softly in the snow. But the glass case had shattered and the face and hands were crumpled and bent out of all recognition. Even the jewels had flown and lay twinkling in the snow.

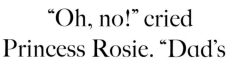

"Oh, no!" cried Princess Rosie. "Dad's beautiful present is ruined, and I haven't got any gold left to buy him another one." She dug in her pocket and pulled out the tiny bronze coin that the man in the shop had given her.

"This isn't enough for a mince pie, let alone a lovely present," she groaned. Then Princess Rosie did the only thing she could think of. She sat beside the fountain and cried. She was crying so loudly that she didn't notice Jack, the stable boy, until he was standing right beside her.

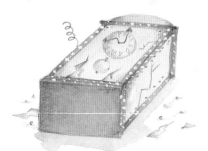

"What's wrong, Princess Rosie?" asked Jack kindly.

"I bought my dad a wonderful present, then I dropped it, and that's all that's left," sobbed Rosie. She pointed towards the shattered remains of the clock lying in the snow. "Now I've got nothing to give him for Christmas. And I really wanted to give him a special present to show him how much I love him."

"Oh, dear," said Jack, carefully picking up the broken bits of clock. "I'll tell you what. Why don't you come back to my place and I'll see if I can fix it for you."

Princess Rosie couldn't see how a stable boy thought he was going to fix the clock, but she felt she had no other choice, so she decided to go with him.

Jack led Rosie up some steps to a room above the stables. As Jack swung the door open, Rosie closed her eyes and took a deep breath. She hoped it wasn't going to be too dirty and smelly.

But when she opened her eyes, she was pleasantly surprised. The room was bright and as neat as a pin. It was even decorated in festive strips of holly and ivy. But best of all, there was a tree in the corner covered with lovely things.

"What are all these things?" asked Rosie. She went over to the tree and stroked a carved wooden horse.

"Oh, they're the Christmas presents I've made for my family," explained Jack shyly. "The horse is for my dad. He loves horses, just like me. The knitted gloves are for my mum. She always gets cold hands, especially when we make snowmen on Christmas Day. And the wooden flute and tin whistle are for my brother and sister."

Princess Rosie was amazed. Each present was beautifully made and really thoughtful. While Jack tried to put the clock back together, he told Rosie how he spent his evenings making the gifts.

"They might not be grand," he laughed, "but each and every one of them is made with love."

As Jack said the word "love", Princess Rosie sat bolt upright. He had given her an idea. She could make her dad a present to show him how much she loved him. She jumped to her feet and thanked Jack for trying to fix the clock.

"If you give me a few days I think I can fix it," he said.

"No, don't worry," she cried. "You keep it." She was just about to leave the room when she turned around and gave Jack a hug. "You've saved my Christmas," she smiled, and she gave him a kiss on the cheek. Jack blushed from head to foot.

"But what have I done?" asked Jack, looking confused.

"Don't worry. You've helped solve my present problem," laughed Princess Rosie, as she raced down the steps.

Back at the palace, Princess Rosie rushed straight to a cupboard in the schoolroom. She rummaged around until she found what she was looking for - paints, a paintbrush and some crisp white paper.

Then she got to work painting a picture of herself and her dad building a snowman. They'd never actually built a snowman together - after all, it wasn't the sort of thing that kings and princesses did - but Rosie thought it would be a nice thing to do.

Rosie painted all afternoon and into the evening. By dinnertime the painting was finished, and she left it to dry while she ate.

After dinner, Rosie took the painting to the royal carpenter's workshop, and he showed her how to make a frame for it to go in. After that, Rosie just had time to wrap it up before her dad appeared and told her it was bedtime.

Rosie was very excited when she awoke the next morning. It was Christmas Day, and she couldn't wait to give her present to her dad. But before she had even jumped out of her bed, her dad came into her room.

"I'm afraid your present couldn't wait any longer," he laughed, as he produced a wriggling ball of fluff from behind his back.

"Oh," gasped Princess Rosie. It was a ginger kitten. She took it from her dad and hugged it to her chest.

"Thank you, thank you, thank you," she gushed. "I'll call him Duke. Now can I give you your present?"

"I'm afraid I haven't got time, Rosie," said the king. "I've got all the official gifts to open before breakfast. If I start now, I might be finished in an hour or two. Hurry down when you're ready and you can watch me."

71

Princess Rosie quickly got dressed and rushed down to the throne room with Duke in one arm and her dad's present in the other.

Rosie's dad was surrounded by magnificent gifts. "And this one," said his chief adviser, holding out an ornate clock a lot like the one that Rosie had bought him, "is from the Earl of Kevil."

"Please put it with the other clocks," said the king, waving a weary hand towards a row of more jewel-encrusted clocks.

"And this is from the Queen of Inmarsh," said the chief adviser. He placed a diamond-studded music box in the king's hands.

The king glanced at the pile of expensive gifts and gave a heavy sigh. "Are there many more?" he asked.

"Just these," said the adviser, handing the king a matching crown and sceptre.

"Put them with the other crown jewels," said the king, barely looking at them. "Is that the last of the presents?" he asked eagerly.

"Er, not quite," whispered Princess Rosie. She chewed her lips nervously. If her dad was so bored by all those splendid gifts, what would he think of her silly old painting? Perhaps she wouldn't give it to him, after all.

She tried to hide the present behind her back, but it was no use. The king had seen it.

"Have you got a present for me, Rosie?" he asked. "Come on, don't be shy."

Princess Rosie edged forwards and shyly handed her present to her dad. "It's not much. I made it myself," she whispered.

Then she buried her face in Duke's fur so she didn't have to watch her dad open the present. Silence fell over the throne room, and Rosie wished that the ground would open up and swallow her.

Then, one by one, the king's advisers and the rest of the court began to clap. Rosie wondered what was going on. She peeked out from behind Duke and blinked in surprise. Her dad had a very big, very un-kinglike grin on his face.

"This is the best, most thoughtful present I've ever received," he cried. "Come here, Rosie, give your old dad a kiss."

Rosie rushed up to her dad and he gave her a big hug. "I love you, Daddy," she whispered in his ear.

"And I love you, too," he whispered back.

Then he turned to his chief adviser. "Please hang this painting over my throne," he said.

"Then tell Cook that Princess Rosie and the king are going to be late for breakfast. We're going outside to build a snowman. Merry Christmas, everyone!"

JINGLE BELLS

Dashing through the snow,
In a one-horse open sleigh,
O'er the fields we go,
Laughing all the way.
Bells on bob-tail ring,
Making spirits bright;
What fun it is to ride and sing
A sleighing song tonight!

Chorus: Jingle bells, jingle bells,
Jingle all the way;
Oh, what fun it is to ride
In a one-horse open sleigh.
Oh, jingle bells, jingle bells,
Jingle all the way;
Oh, what fun it is to ride
In a one-horse open sleigh!

THE RAINBOW
SNOWMAN

"Hooray! It snowed!" cried Joshua, as he opened the curtains one morning. His sister Olivia rushed to the bedroom window.

"Wow!" she exclaimed. "It's really deep! Let's go to the park and build a snowman."

The two children got dressed as quickly as they could and rushed downstairs.

"Can we take this old hat and scarf for our snowman, Mum?" asked Olivia.

Mum smiled. "Of course," she said. "You can have my old skiing gloves, too."

Olivia and Joshua ran all the way to the park, making crazy footprint trails on the pavement all the way.

"Let's build our snowman right next to the Christmas tree by the bandstand," suggested Joshua. "Then he can join in the carol concert tonight."

"Yes!" agreed Olivia. "If we dress him up in these bright clothes, everyone will notice him!"

The two children got to work. Using their feet, they scooped up a huge mound of fresh snow. Next they piled armfuls of snow on top, patting it down with their gloved hands, until the mound was almost up to Joshua's shoulders.

"Now for the head," panted Olivia. She squeezed together a snowball and rolled it down the slope. Over and over it tumbled, gathering snow as it went. Bigger and bigger it grew, until Olivia and Joshua had to push it on their hands and knees.

"It MUST be big enough now!" puffed Olivia, brushing the snow off her wet knees. "We won't be able to lift it if it grows any more!"

Together, the two children hoisted the giant snowball into the air. PLONK! They placed it firmly on top of the snow mound. Olivia stuck spiky sticks in for the arms, while Joshua made the face with two pebbles, a twig and a carrot. Finally, they dressed their snowman in the bright orange hat, red gloves and the long, multi-coloured scarf.

"He looks great!" laughed Olivia. "He must be the most colourful snowman in town – and he knows it! It looks like he's smiling!"

Just then, the town clock struck twelve. "Lunchtime!" cried Joshua, patting his rumbling tummy. "I thought I was feeling hungry."

"Me too," agreed his sister. "Let's go home. It's cold."

Olivia and Joshua waved their snowman goodbye. "Bye!" they shouted. "We'll be back for the carol concert tonight."

It was cold in the park, and getting colder all the time. As the afternoon went on, the sun dipped lower and lower in the sky. Soon the snowy ground began to freeze. The park emptied until finally the snowman was left all alone, with just the shivering park animals for company.

"I hope our snowman is all right," said Joshua, as he and Olivia sat at home, eating warm soup. "It's freezing out there."

"He'll be fine," said Mum. "Snowmen don't mind the cold. Anyway, he's got all those colourful clothes to keep him warm."

But that was where their mum was wrong. It's true that snowmen don't mind the cold. After all, they are made of snow. But Joshua and Olivia's snowman didn't have an orange hat any more, or a striped scarf, or even a pair of red gloves. All his clothes were gone!

The orange hat was now a cosy nest for the shivering birds...

The holey red gloves had become beds for a family of mice...

And the long, multi-coloured scarf? It made a perfect lining for the rabbits' burrow in the frozen ground.

That evening, when Joshua and Olivia arrived at the park for the carol concert, they wriggled their way to the front of the crowd.

"Mum! Dad! Come and see our colourful snowman!" they pointed. But of course, the snowman wasn't colourful any more. He was as plain and white as any ordinary snowman.

"OH!" cried Olivia and Joshua in disappointment. "Where are his clothes? No one will notice him now!"

Just then, the crowd fell silent. The mayor had arrived to turn on the Christmas tree lights and start the carol concert.

"THREE, TWO, ONE! MERRY CHRISTMAS!"
roared the mayor, as he flicked the switch. In an instant, the
Christmas tree lit up like magic, casting coloured light over
the snow.

"WOW!" cried Olivia and Joshua in unison. "Look at our
snowman!" The snowman was glowing like a rainbow.

"Oooh!" gasped the crowd. "Look at the rainbow
snowman! Isn't he amazing? And look at that smile! He must
be the happiest snowman in town."

And do you know, he WAS the happiest snowman in town.

SILENT NIGHT

Silent night! Holy night!
All is calm, all is bright.
Round yon virgin mother and child,
Holy infant so tender and mild,
Sleep in heavenly peace!
Sleep in heavenly peace!

Silent night! Holy night!
Shepherds quake at the sight;
Glories stream from heaven afar,
Heavenly hosts sing Alleluia,
Christ, the Saviour, is born!
Christ, the Saviour, is born!

Silent night! Holy night!
Son of God, love's pure light
Radiant beams from Thy Holy face,
With the dawn of redeeming grace,
Jesus, Lord, at Thy birth,
Jesus, Lord, at Thy birth.

To Santa Claus
North Pole

THE MAGICAL
SLEIGH RIDE

Once upon a time, in a faraway land, there lived a little girl called Tansy. Tansy lived with her mum, dad, little brother Daniel, and her beloved grandma. Tansy and her family were very happy. The land where they lived was beautiful and bright. The sun always shone, it seldom rained, and it was never, ever cold.

Sometimes, when Tansy was tucked up in bed, her grandmother would tell her tales about the chilly lands in the North where she had lived as a girl. Tansy loved hearing about her grandma's homeland, and her favourite stories were the ones about snow.

"Sometimes it would snow all night long and I would wake up to a crispy white world," Grandma would tell her. "When you walked on the snow, it would crunch beneath your feet and you would leave perfect footprints behind you. And it was really soft. You could pick it up and squeeze it to make snowballs. Then you threw them at your friends."

"It must have been fun," laughed Tansy.

"It was," smiled Grandma, "but my favourite thing was when it snowed on Christmas Day. We would make a snowman before breakfast, then go inside and warm our freezing hands by the fire."

"I would love snow on Christmas Day," sighed Tansy.

One day, not long before Christmas, Tansy had an idea. "Let's write a letter to Santa," she said to Daniel, "asking him if we can have snow on Christmas Day."

Daniel thought it was a brilliant idea. So Tansy wrote a letter to Santa Claus in her best handwriting. It read:

Dear Santa,
I live in a sunny land and I have never seen snow before. My grandma says snow is so cold you can make snowballs and snowmen out of it. Can I please have some snow for Christmas? My brother would like some too.
                              Love from Tansy x

When Tansy had finished, she and Daniel both signed the letter and then put it in an envelope. On the outside of the envelope Tansy wrote...

To Santa Claus
North Pole

Grandma gave them a stamp, and then they mailed it straight away.

A week before Christmas, Tansy's dad brought the Christmas tree down from the attic and the children got to work decorating it. They covered it with balls made of fluffy cotton and put a shining star on top.

Then Tansy went outside. Grandma had told her that before it snows the whole sky is covered with a grey cloud. Tansy looked up. The sky was a clear blue and the sun shone bright and hot. There wasn't a cloud anywhere.

"I wonder if Santa got my letter," she whispered to herself. "Maybe he's looking at it now and getting the snow ready to bring to us on Christmas Day."

All that week Tansy kept looking at the sky, waiting for the clouds, but every day the sky was blue and the sun shone brightly.

On Christmas Eve the children went to bed early. Tansy found it hard to get to sleep. She was so excited at the thought of waking up on Christmas morning and finding snow that she didn't feel sleepy at all.

She wondered how Santa would bring the snow. Would he bring it in a sack the same way he brought the presents? She started to worry that when he brought the snow the hot sun would melt it before she had a chance to see it.

Tansy lay in bed tossing and turning. Suddenly she heard a noise. It sounded like bells tinkling in the night sky.

She got up and looked out of the window. It had become dark suddenly, but in the moonlight, on the grass below, she could see some strange animals.

Tansy remembered seeing some like them on a Christmas card and realized they must be Santa's reindeer. They were harnessed to a brightly painted sleigh. Next to them, dressed all in red, his face almost covered by a long white beard, was Santa Claus!

When he saw Tansy, Santa waved. "Hurry up, Tansy," he called. "We're going on a magical journey. Go and get Daniel."

Tansy woke her brother. "Come quickly," she whispered excitedly. "Santa's here!"

Tansy and Daniel quickly dressed and ran into the garden. Santa was waiting for them, with a huge smile on his face.

"Come," he said, holding out his hands. "I have something for you." And he gave each of the children a bundle of warm clothes. "They're for later, when it starts to get cold," he explained.

"Where's the snow, Santa?" asked Daniel.

"I can't bring the snow to you," chuckled Santa. "It would only melt in the sun. So you're going to the snow! Now, giddy-up, my trusty reindeer!" he cried. "Fly as fast as you can!"

The children held on tightly as the reindeer leaped into the air, pulling the sleigh behind them. Higher and higher they climbed, until the ground was far below them. Then the sleigh straightened up, and soon they were flying along beneath the stars. The magical sleigh ride had begun...

They flew over forests and rivers, jagged
mountaintops, and sandy deserts. Sometimes all the
children could see was mile upon mile of dark countryside,
and then the blackness would be broken as they passed
over big cities scattered with a million lights.

"Now put on your warm clothes," Santa told them. "We're nearly there."

After a few minutes the sleigh landed. The children looked around in amazement. The whole world was completely white. Hills, fields, trees and houses were all covered in what looked like powdery, white sugar. Everything sparkled like diamonds in the moonlight.

Tansy took off one of her gloves and touched the snow with a finger. It was just as Grandma had described it. Soft and yet firm, dry and yet wet. And it was very, very cold.

A door opened in a house nearby and the children saw a smiling woman standing in the doorway.

"Welcome to the North Pole, children," she smiled. "I'm Mrs Claus."

For the next few hours the children had a wonderful time. Santa introduced them to his helpers and showed them the workshop where the toys were made.

Then came the best part of all...playing in the snow.

They made trails of footprints. Next they had a snowball fight.

And, of course, they made a snowman. They used two of Santa's spare black buttons for eyes and a carrot for his nose. Tansy wrapped her new scarf around his neck and Daniel put his woolly hat on his head. Then everybody held hands and danced around him, singing a song:

"I'm a jolly snowman round and neat.
I've got no hands and got no feet.
I like the cold but not the heat
Seeing you is such a treat."

They danced and sang until they could dance no more. Then they went inside the house and warmed themselves by the fire. The children were so comfortable that their eyes started to close, and soon they were fast asleep.

When Tansy awoke it was morning. She was in her own bed, in her own bedroom. The curtains were open and the sun was shining, but there was no snow outside. Everything looked the same as usual.

Tansy remembered her night-time adventure. Had it all been a dream? It had felt so real. Meeting Santa. The journey in the sleigh. Dancing around the snowman. She could even remember the song they had sung.

Feeling a bit confused, she quickly got dressed and went downstairs.

"Merry Christmas, Tansy," Grandma said, handing her a small package. It was round and hard and was wrapped in snowflake-covered paper. On a little label it said, "To Tansy. Love, Santa x."

Tansy opened the present carefully. Inside was a beautiful glass ball filled with snow – it was a snow-globe. Inside there were two children and three elves dancing around a snowman. Her heart gave a leap. So it hadn't been a dream, after all!

Tansy shook the globe and it began to play a familiar tune. "It's our snowman song," laughed Tansy. "And that's us, dancing around the snowman, just like we did last night."

Tansy's parents and grandma stared at the globe in amazement.

"How did you get in there?" asked Dad.

"You'd have to ask Santa that. But I do know he gave us what we asked for," laughed Tansy. "Snow on Christmas Day!"

Deck the Halls

Deck the halls with boughs of holly,
Fa la la la la, la la la la.
'Tis the season to be jolly,
Fa la la la la, la la la la.
Don we now our gay apparel,
Fa la la, la la la, la la la.
Troll the ancient Yuletide carol,
Fa la la la la, la la la la.

See the blazing Yule before us,
Fa la la la la, la la la la.
Strike the harp and join the chorus,
Fa la la la la, la la la la.
Follow me in merry measure,
Fa la la, la la la, la la la.
While I tell a Yuletide treasure,
Fa la la la la, la la la la.

Fast away the old year passes,
Fa la la la la, la la la la.
Hail the new, ye lads and lasses,
Fa la la la la, la la la la.
Sing we joyous, all together,
Fa la la, la la la, la la la.
Heedless of the wind and weather,
Fa la la la la, la la la la.

A Special
Job for Clyde

Christmas was coming and everyone in Santa's workshop was busy. Everyone, that is, except for Clyde.

Clyde was looking for something to do. He'd been sent out of the workshop for breaking three bicycles in a row. The reindeer had shooed him away after he'd spilled dirty water all over their nice clean stable. Even Mrs Claus had told him to go away after he had sat on a tray of freshly baked mince pies.

"There must be something I can do," said Clyde out loud.

"Why don't you go outside and count snowflakes," said Edward, the eldest elf.

So Clyde stomped out into the snow and started to count. "One, two, three... oops! Was that four or five?" Clyde started counting again. "One, two, three, eight..." Clyde tried his best to count all the snowflakes, but it was no use. There were just too many. He began to race around in circles grabbing handfuls of snow.

Clyde was so busy counting that he didn't notice Santa Claus until he ran straight into him and bounced off his large, round belly.

"Steady, Clyde!" laughed Santa. "What are you up to?"

Clyde scrambled to his feet. "I'm counting the snowflakes," he explained. "It's a very important job."

Then, as he saw a smile spread across Santa's face, Clyde had a terrible thought. Counting snowflakes wasn't an important job at all. It was just a way of keeping him out of everyone's way. Clyde was so upset that tears filled his eyes.

"What's wrong?" asked Santa.

"N...n...nothing," mumbled Clyde, turning away so that Santa couldn't see his tears. Poor old Clyde didn't notice the huge tree just behind him and crashed right into it.

"Ahhh!" he cried, as a huge pile of snow slipped off the tree and thumped on his head. Clyde scrambled to his feet and looked around. Where was Santa Claus? Then he noticed something red poking out of the snow. It was Santa's hat! Santa Claus was buried in a landslide of snow – a landslide that Clyde had caused!

Clyde got down on his hands and knees and began to dig quickly. Santa was soon free.

"I'm so sorry," gasped Clyde. "I really am a terrible clf. I'm so clumsy that I spoil everything. I don't blame the other elves for not wanting me in the workshop. I should just leave the North Pole." And he sat down and started to cry.

"Don't cry, Clyde," said Santa. "It's Christmas, and Christmas is a time for laughter and happiness, not tears and sadness."

"But everyone would be much happier if I wasn't around. After all, what good is an elf who breaks toys instead of making them?" sobbed Clyde.

As Clyde spoke, Santa Claus began to smile. "Come with me," he said, helping Clyde to his feet. "I've got the perfect job for you. And it really is an important one."

Santa led Clyde back to the workshop and took him into a room that he'd never seen before.

"This," said Santa grandly, "is Quality Control, or QC for short. It is where all the toys are tested to make sure they are strong enough for the little boys and girls to play with on Christmas Day. I've been looking for the right elf to put in charge of it, and I think you might be that elf."

"But why me?" asked Clyde. He picked up a teddy bear and began to fiddle with it nervously. "Oops!" he cried, as the bear's head fell off.

Much to Clyde's surprise, Santa smiled happily.

"See, I knew you were the elf for the job. If the toys aren't strong enough for you to play with, they won't be strong enough for children to play with. And we can't have broken toys on Christmas Day."

"But what about the broken toys?" asked Clyde.

"You'll have to send them back to the workshop to be repaired. That way, all the toys that are opened on Christmas Day will be strong and good," smiled Santa.

"Wow," laughed Clyde. "I think you are right. I am just the elf for this job!"

And from that day on, Clyde worked hard making sure that only the best toys ever left the North Pole. Clyde was happy, and Santa Claus and the other elves were happy. Best of all, on Christmas Day, all the little children were happy, too.

O Little Town
of Bethlehem

O little town of Bethlehem, how still we see thee lie.
Above thy deep and dreamless sleep the silent stars go by.
Yet in thy dark streets shineth the everlasting light,
The hopes and fears of all the years are met in thee tonight.

For Christ is born of Mary, and gathered all above,
While mortals sleep, the angels keep their watch of
wondering love.
Oh morning stars together proclaim the holy birth
And praises sing to God the king, and peace to men on earth.

How silently, how silently the wondrous gift is given.
So God imparts to human hearts the blessings of his heaven.
No ear may hear his coming, but in this world of sin,
Where meek souls will receive him still, the dear Christ enters in.

Oh holy Child of Bethlehem, descend to us we pray.
Cast out our sin and enter in, be born in us today.
We hear the Christmas angels the great glad tidings tell.
O come to us, abide with us, our lord Emmanuel.

THE LITTLE
CHRISTMAS TREE

It was Christmas Eve. Tom was lying on his bed reading a comic when he heard a CRASH, followed by someone shouting "OUCH!" in a very loud voice.

"Hurry up, Tom!" called his dad up the stairs. "I need help with something."

What on earth was he doing? Tom jumped off his bed and raced downstairs to go and see. There, wedged in the doorway, was a giant Christmas tree, with two legs sticking out from underneath it.

"I seem to be a bit stuck," said Dad's voice. "Can you get Mum?" Tom soon returned with his mum.

"It's kind of, umm, big," she said, trying not to giggle. She and Tom took hold of one end of the tree. One, two, three, PUSH. For a brief moment, the tree stuck fast, then WHOOSH! It slid through the open doorway and landed on the hallway floor – along with Dad. OOF!

"What do you think?" asked Dad, standing the giant tree upright against the wall. "Isn't it magnificent?"

"It's enormous!" laughed Tom. "Where are we going to put it?"

"Where we always put the Christmas tree," replied Dad. "In the kitchen, of course."

"OH!" said Tom, looking puzzled. "But what about the little Christmas tree in the attic? We always put that up in the kitchen."

"Not any more. We're having a REAL tree this year," said Dad. "Just smell that fresh pine!"

"It IS time we got rid of that shabby little tree," agreed Mum. "Some of the parts were missing last year."

Tom's face fell. "But I don't want a big tree," he protested. "I want our little old tree. We ALWAYS put it up on Christmas Eve."

"Sorry, Tom," said Dad, looking uncomfortable. "I put it outside by the back door for the dustman. It's probably in the back of a rubbish van by now."

Tom rushed round to the back door, his heart pounding. He couldn't stand the thought of the little tree sitting in a rubbish van full of smelly, rotten food.

Thank goodness! The tattered old box containing the Christmas tree was still there, looking very sad.

"Can't we keep it?" Tom begged his parents. "Pleeease? I could put it in my bedroom," he suggested.

Mum smiled. "Oh, all right," she laughed.

Tom carried the box up the stairs to his room. He got to work putting together the old Christmas tree. It took ages, especially since there were so many parts missing. But when he was finished, the little tree really didn't look so bad. Of course, it didn't have all its branches, but if you turned it around, you couldn't tell – well not from the front, anyway.

"All we need now are decorations," he told the little tree. "Then you'll look great!"

"May I please have some Christmas decorations for my tree?" asked Tom that lunchtime.

"Of course," replied his dad. "Let's see what's left over when we've decorated the big tree. I thought we could do it this afternoon."

"Fantastic!" cried Tom. Now that the little tree was safe in his room, he felt excited about having a tree that almost touched the roof.

Dad and Tom cleared the table while his mum got the Christmas decorations out of the cupboard.

"I hope there will be enough for both trees," said Mum, peering inside the box. "Our old tree was MUCH smaller."

But Tom wasn't listening. He was already rummaging through the box of glittering decorations, searching for his favourites.

"These long glass icicles will look fantastic on the big tree!" he cried, dangling them in the light.

It was almost dinnertime when the giant tree was finally finished. Tom and his parents stood back to admire their work.

"Magnificent!" said Dad.

"Wonderful!" said Mum.

"Super!" added Tom. "May I have the rest of the decorations?" He scooped up the box, ready to take it upstairs. "OH!" he exclaimed in disappointment. "It's empty!"

"Sorry, Tom," said Dad. "We seem to have used all the decorations on the big tree. We might just have enough time to buy some more before the shops close."

Just then, a horn honked outside in the driveway.

"That must be Grandma and Grandpa," said Mum, cleverly changing the subject. "Why don't you go out and see, Tom?"

Tom loved it when his grandparents came to stay. They were always full of good ideas for things to do – and they NEVER got angry.

"Grandma! Grandpa!" cried Tom, waving at their red car. "Come and see our enormous Christmas tree. It's amazing!"

Grandma and Grandpa bustled in through the front door, carrying armfuls of brightly wrapped Christmas presents.

"Is the tree in the kitchen again?" asked Grandma. "Just let me put these presents under it, Tom. Then I can take a proper look!"

Grandma added her packages to the large stack already under the tree, and stood up.

"Goodness!" she chuckled, putting on her glasses to inspect the giant fir more closely. "It really is a whopper!"

She turned to Tom. "What happened to the sweet little tree you usually have?"

In the excitement of his grandparents' arrival, Tom had
forgotten all about the little tree.

"Oh!" he cried. "It's up in my bedroom. I was going
to decorate it this afternoon, but there weren't enough
decorations for both trees … and now all the shops will
be closed."

A cloud came over Tom's face. How could he have forgotten about the little tree? Now it wouldn't be decorated for Christmas Day!

"Don't worry," said Grandpa, putting his arm around Tom's shoulder. "I just happen to know how to make terrific Christmas tree decorations out of nothing but tinfoil, glue, and some glitter."

"You're the best Grandpa!" replied a happy, and very relieved, Tom.

Later that evening Tom and his grandpa sat down at the kitchen table. Grandpa crumpled up pieces of tinfoil into balls, and Tom painted them with glue and sprinkled glitter on them.

"Those will look wonderful on your little tree," said Grandma admiringly. "Really sparkly! Have you looked out of the window, Tom?"

Tom pulled back the curtains and grinned.

"Look, Grandpa!" he cried excitedly. "It's snowing!"

Heavy flakes were falling thick and fast through the night sky, covering the ground in a white blanket.

"Well, I never," whistled Grandpa. "Looks like we're going to have a white Christmas this year. It will freeze tonight, too, if I'm not mistaken. Poor birds!"

"What do you mean, 'poor birds'?" asked Tom. "Don't they like the snow? I love it!"

"It's not so much the snow," explained Grandpa. "It's when the ground and water freezes. Then there's very little food or water around. It makes life very hard for the birds, you know."

"Oh!" said Tom, looking concerned. "I never really thought of that. Can't WE give them something to eat and drink?"

"Of course," replied Grandpa. "That's why people have bird feeders in their gardens. They put out fresh food and water every morning."

"We don't have a bird feeder," said Tom. "I know!" he cried. "Let's use my little tree instead! We can decorate it with bits of food and put it in the garden. It can be our Christmas present to the birds!"

"Great idea, Tom!" cried Grandpa. "We'd better get started straight away, if it's going to be ready for the morning!"

When Mum, Dad, and Grandma heard Tom's plan, they thought it was a wonderful idea.

"I'll make some mesh bags to hang on the branches," offered Grandma. "You can fill them with some nuts and pieces of coconut."

"What about these scraps of bacon rind and fat?" suggested Mum. "The birds love them. And cheese, too."

Soon Tom had a host of goodies to hang on his special little tree.

"Don't forget to hang our sparkly foil decorations on it, too," reminded Grandpa. "Then it will look really festive!"

Grandma helped Tom wrap some silver paper around the battered old pot, and tie a large bow on the front. Then the whole family decorated the branches with nut bags, foil balls, bacon rind and all the other goodies.

"I don't think there's room for even one more thing!" laughed Tom, as he hung the last nut bag on the tree.

Tom and his grandparents watched from his
bedroom window as his dad carefully carried the little
tree into the garden and placed it in the middle of the white,
snow-covered lawn.

"Everyone else might think it's a shabby old tree," yawned Tom, as he climbed into bed, "but I think it looks great. I hope the birds like it, too."

"They'll love it!" whispered Grandma, leaning over to give him a hug. But Tom didn't hear. He was already fast asleep.

The next morning was Christmas Day.

"WHOOPEE!" yelled Tom, leaping out of bed and racing down the stairs, two steps at a time.

"Merry Christmas, everyone! Did Santa come?"

"Of course!" laughed his parents. "Your presents are under the Christmas tree."

At the mention of Christmas trees, Tom suddenly remembered his present for the birds. He ran to the window and looked out into the garden.

"WOW!" he shouted, opening the window. "Come and see, everyone!"

There in the middle of the lawn stood the little Christmas tree. No one could describe it as shabby today. Its frosted boughs twinkled in the morning light. Never in all its days as a Christmas tree had it looked so lovely – or so busy. It was surrounded by twittering birds, all fighting over the food.

"I think they like their Christmas present," laughed Grandpa. "All the food will be gone before the day is out. You'll have to load up the branches again."

"Oh, yes!" cried Tom. "But it's not just for Christmas. The birds will need to be fed every day, until the warmer weather comes. And that way, we HAVE to keep our little tree. Fantastic!"

THE TWELVE DAYS OF CHRISTMAS

On the first day of Christmas,
My true love gave to me:
A partridge in a pear tree.

On the second day of Christmas,
My true love gave to me:
Two turtledoves,
And a partridge in a pear tree.

On the third day of Christmas,
My true love gave to me:
Three French hens,
Two turtledoves,
And a partridge in a pear tree.

On the fourth day of Christmas,
My true love gave to me:
Four calling birds,
Three French hens,
Two turtledoves,
And a partridge in a pear tree.

On the fifth day of Christmas,
My true love gave to me:
Five golden rings!
Four calling birds,
Three French hens,
Two turtledoves,
And a partridge in a pear tree.

On the sixth day of Christmas,
My true love gave to me:
Six geese a-laying,
Five golden rings!
Four calling birds,
Three French hens,
Two turtledoves,
And a partridge in a pear tree.

On the seventh day of Christmas,
My true love gave to me:
Seven swans a-swimming,
Six geese a-laying,
Five golden rings!
Four calling birds,
Three French hens,
Two turtledoves,
And a partridge in a pear tree.

On the eighth day of Christmas,
My true love gave to me:
Eight maids a-milking,
Seven swans a-swimming,
Six geese a-laying,
Five golden rings!
Four calling birds,
Three French hens,
Two turtledoves,
And a partridge in a pear tree.

On the ninth day of Christmas,
My true love gave to me:
Nine ladies dancing,
Eight maids a-milking,
Seven swans a-swimming,
Six geese a-laying,
Five golden rings!
Four calling birds,
Three French hens,
Two turtledoves,
And a partridge in a pear tree.

On the tenth day of Christmas,
My true love gave to me:
Ten lords a-leaping,
Nine ladies dancing,
Eight maids a-milking,
Seven swans a-swimming,
Six geese a-laying,
Five golden rings!
Four calling birds,
Three French hens,
Two turtledoves,
And a partridge in a pear tree.

On the eleventh day of Christmas,
My true love gave to me:
Eleven pipers piping,
Ten lords a-leaping,
Nine ladies dancing,
Eight maids a-milking,
Seven swans a-swimming,
Six geese a-laying,
Five golden rings!
Four calling birds,
Three French hens,
Two turtledoves,
And a partridge in a pear tree.

On the twelfth day of Christmas,
My true love gave to me:
Twelve drummers drumming,
Eleven pipers piping,
Ten lords a-leaping,
Nine ladies dancing,
Eight maids a-milking,
Seven swans a-swimming,
Six geese a-laying,
Five golden rings!
Four calling birds,
Three French hens,
Two turtledoves,
And a partridge in a pear tree.

CHRISTABEL'S CHRISTMAS WISH

Have you ever lost something, then found it again when you were least expecting to?

Have you ever thought something was broken, only to find that it worked later? You might think it was just luck – but you'd be wrong. It was a house fairy at work!

There are house fairies in every home – though you will never see them. They are experts at hiding. Every day, they flutter about the house, secretly finding and mending things, sweeping up biscuit crumbs, and doing all the little jobs that busy humans forget to do. And their busiest time of the year? You've guessed it – Christmas!

Fairies have to be at their most alert at Christmas time, because that's when they're most likely to get caught. And everyone knows that fairies must be kept secret...

Twins Chloe and Oliver Tate had a house fairy in their house, though they didn't know it for sure. They couldn't help noticing that odd things sometimes happened in their home.

"Mum, did YOU find Teddy for me?" asked Chloe one day.

"No," Mum replied. "I didn't know he was lost."

"Then how did he get back on my pillow?" she wondered. It was a mystery.

There were other things too, like the neat little stitches in Oliver's holey socks, and what looked like tiny footprints on their dusty bookshelf.

"I'm sure we've got a fairy in this house," Oliver told his parents, as they examined a fresh trail of prints one morning.

Mum and Dad laughed. "That would be lovely!" Mum said, but Oliver and Chloe could tell that they didn't really believe them.

Chloe and Oliver weren't so sure. "Thank you!" they always whispered when they went to bed at night...just in case a fairy was listening.

A fairy WAS listening. A very tiny, hard-working house fairy called Christabel. Christabel had been in Chloe and Oliver's house ever since it was built. She had watched lots of children grow up there over the years, but the twins were her favourites.

"How lovely to be thanked!" she would think, when she heard their words each night. And they had something else in common. They all loved Christmas. It was Christmas in two weeks' time. If only she could share it with them!

"I wish we could talk together and be friends. It does get so lonely in this big old house sometimes," she thought to herself sadly.

Of course, Christabel knew that talking to the children was impossible. House fairies must NEVER be seen by humans. But it didn't stop her from wishing.

One night, just before Christmas, Christabel overheard the twins talking with their dad.

"Dad, please can we get the decorations down from the attic tomorrow?" begged Oliver.

Dad nodded. "And we can put up the Christmas tree, too. It's nearly Christmas Eve."

"Hooray!" cried the twins, hopping around in excitement. "That's our favourite job!"

Christabel couldn't help smiling. Sorting out the Christmas decorations was her favourite job, too. "I'd better tie some new silver thread on the baubles tonight," she thought to herself. "I must clean the tinsel, too. It looked rather dusty last year." And off she fluttered to the attic, to search for the box of decorations.

She found it in a corner, along with a bag of old Christmas wrapping paper and bows. The box was filled with a tangle of twinkling tinsel and glittering decorations.

"How I wish I was a Christmas fairy so I could share Christmas Day with Chloe and Oliver," Christabel sighed as she began to untangle the colourful mess. "It really is no fun on my own."

One by one, Christabel lifted the delicate baubles out of the box, and laid them on a cushion. First she gave them a quick dusting by gently flapping her wings. Then she neatly knotted a new loop of silver thread on each one, before sprinkling it with fairy dust and replacing it in the box.

"Just a little extra magic sparkle to make the tree really special!" she smiled to herself.

Next, Christabel got to work on the tinsel. She hung it all across the attic, and danced all the way along each tinsel string, shaking off the dust. By the time she had finished, the hard-working house fairy was tired out – and covered in dust from head to toe!

"Look at my wings and my dress," she sighed, trying to brush it off. "It's a good job no one ever sees me. I always look so grubby!"

The next morning, the twins were awake bright and early. They couldn't wait to decorate the tree.

"Here you are, Chloe," said Dad, passing down the box of decorations from the attic. "You can start by putting some new loops on the baubles. Oliver, you can dust the tinsel."

Chloe opened the box and looked inside. "That's strange," she exclaimed in surprise, showing the baubles to Oliver. "They've already got new loops. Mum must have done it."

Oliver gave the tinsel a quick shake. "Not much dust this year either," he said, frowning at Chloe. "That's strange."

"Your fairy must have been at work!" joked Dad. "Come on, you two. Let's get started."

Chloe and Oliver glanced around suspiciously, before following their dad downstairs. "I wonder..." they whispered under their breath.

Chloe and Oliver spent all afternoon putting up the decorations with their parents. First they hung Christmas cards along ribbons on the wall, and tinsel round the fireplace. Then they made long multi-coloured paper chains to string across the living room.

"That looks great," cried Chloe. "Now for the best job – decorating the tree!"

One by one, Chloe and Oliver hung the decorations on the tree, while Mum draped silvery strands on the branches.

Finally, there was just a large golden star left. Dad climbed up the ladder and fixed it to the very top, before curling the Christmas lights in between the branches.

"Are you ready?" he asked. CLICK! He flicked on the Christmas light switch. Everyone gasped.

"It looks beautiful!" cried Chloe and Oliver together.

"It certainly does!" agreed Dad. "Your fairy must have sprinkled a bit of magic dust! Come on, now, you two. It's time for bed."

As the twins lay in bed that night, they thought about what their dad had said.

"I know he was only joking," whispered Oliver, "but the tree did look magical. Maybe a fairy DID help make it look so beautiful."

Chloe nodded. "But if there is a fairy in this house, why have we never seen it? I've looked everywhere I can think of. In all the cupboards, under the beds..."

"Are you two still awake?" interrupted Mum, peering around the bedroom door. "It's getting late."

The twins closed their eyes and pretended to go to sleep, until they were sure their mum had gone.

"Maybe our fairy only comes out at night," suggested Chloe. "That would explain why we haven't seen her."

"I bet you're right!" whispered Oliver excitedly. "I think it's time for us to do some investigating."

Somebody else was awake, too. The hard-working little house fairy was busy trying to get all the dust from the attic off her dress and wings.

"I wonder what the Christmas tree looks like?" she thought, as she sat polishing her wings. "I hope my magic sparkles did the trick."

Just then, the clock in the hallway chimed.

"I know," she decided. "I'll go and take a peek. Everyone will be fast asleep in bed by now."

Christabel fluttered down the stairs to the living room and perched on the mantelpiece over the fireplace. She gazed around the room with a smile. Everything looked so cheery and festive.

"If only I could see it all on Christmas Day," she sighed. "It's so dull on my own." Then she had a daring idea. "Maybe I could hide somewhere on Christmas morning, before anyone gets up. Then I could watch the twins open their presents. No one would know if I was very careful."

Suddenly, Christabel heard a creak, and the living room door opened...Quick as a flash, she darted behind one of the Christmas cards to hide.

It was the twins!

"What on earth are Chloe and Oliver doing downstairs in the middle of the night?" wondered Christabel, peeking out to get a better look. She was so busy watching the children, she didn't see the tall candlestick right beside her. Oops! Over it toppled with a loud clatter.

"Who's there?" cried Chloe and Oliver. They just caught sight of a tiny foot before it disappeared behind some tinsel.

"A fairy!" exclaimed Oliver in triumph. "I knew it!"

Chloe crept over to the fireplace. "Please don't be scared," she called softly. "We won't hurt you."

"Oh, dear! Oh, dear!" cried Christabel, fluttering out from behind the card. "I'll be in SO MUCH trouble now!"

"But why?" asked Chloe, looking concerned. "You only knocked over a candlestick. It was an accident."

"It's not the candlestick," sobbed Christabel. "I'm not supposed to be seen. Imagine what it would be like if everybody knew that fairies existed. We'd never get a moment's peace. But sometimes I just get so lonely in this big old house on my own – especially at Christmas…"

"Please don't worry," said Oliver sympathetically. "Chloe and I won't tell anyone we saw you. We promise, we're very good at keeping secrets."

"Thank you," sniffed Christabel, wiping the tiny tears from her cheeks. "You're both very kind. I suppose I'd better go now, before anyone else comes in. It's been lovely talking to you."

"Wait!" cried Chloe suddenly. "I've got an idea. How would you like to join us on Christmas Day? I promise no one will see you. Would that make you happy?"

"Oh, yes!" exclaimed Christabel. "But how?"

"Yes, how?" repeated Oliver.

Chloe grinned. "Come with me and I'll show you both," she said mysteriously. "All you need is a pretty new dress! I've got some Christmas ribbon in my room. It will be perfect for what I have in mind."

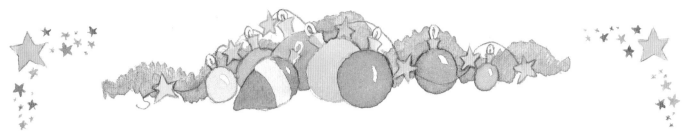

On Christmas morning, Chloe and Oliver couldn't wait for everyone to gather round the Christmas tree after breakfast – and not just because they wanted to open their presents.

"Doesn't our tree look wonderful?" the twins asked Mum and Dad, winking at each other.

"I don't think it's ever looked more beautiful," replied Mum. "It looks magical this year – especially the Christmas fairy on the top. What a beautiful outfit she's wearing. But where did she come from? I don't remember seeing her in the decoration box!"

"Neither do I," said Dad, puzzled. "I thought I put a star at the top of the tree this year. Do you two know where she came from?"

The twins shrugged and smiled mischievously. "Maybe she's one of those fairies you keep talking about," they giggled.

"Maybe she is!" laughed Dad. "Who knows!"

But Chloe and Oliver knew, and so do we!

THE NIGHT BEFORE CHRISTMAS

'Twas the night before Christmas,
When all through the house
Not a creature was stirring, not even a mouse;
The stockings were hung by the chimney with care,
In hopes that St Nicholas soon would be there;
The children were nestled all snug in their beds,
While visions of sugarplums danced in their heads;

And mamma in her 'kerchief, and I in my cap,
Had just settled down for a long winter's nap;
When out on the lawn there arose such a clatter,
I sprang from the bed to see what was the matter.
Away to the window I flew like a flash,
Tore open the shutters and threw up the sash.

The moon, on the breast of the new-fallen snow,
Gave the lustre of midday to objects below,
When, what to my wondering eyes should appear,
But a miniature sleigh, and eight tiny reindeer.
With a little old driver, so lively and quick,
I knew in a moment it must be St Nick.
More rapid than eagles his coursers they came,
And he whistled, and shouted, and called them by name;

"Now, Dasher! Now, Dancer! Now, Prancer and Vixen!
On, Comet! On Cupid! On, Donner and Blitzen!
To the top of the porch! To the top of the wall!
Now dash away! Dash away! Dash away all!"
As dry leaves that before the wild hurricane fly,
When they meet with an obstacle, mount to the sky,
So up to the house-top the coursers they flew,
With the sleigh full of toys, and St Nicholas too.

"Now dash away! Dash away! Dash away all!"

And then, in a twinkling, I heard on the roof
The prancing and pawing of each little hoof;
As I drew in my hand, and was turning around,
Down the chimney St Nicholas came with a bound.

He was dressed all in fur, from his head to his foot,
And his clothes were all tarnished with ashes and soot;
A bundle of toys he had flung on his back,
And he looked like a peddler just opening his pack.

His eyes – how they twinkled! His dimples – how merry!
His cheeks were like roses, his nose like a cherry!
His droll little mouth was drawn up like a bow,
And the beard of his chin was as white as the snow.

He had a broad face and a little round belly,
That shook, when he laughed like a bowlful of jelly;
He was chubby and plump, a right jolly old elf,
And I laughed when I saw him, in spite of myself;
A wink of his eye and a twist of his head,
Soon gave me to know I had nothing to dread.

He spoke not a word, but went straight to his work,
And filled all the stockings; then turned with a jerk;
And laying his finger aside of his nose,
And giving a nod, up the chimney he rose.

He sprang to his sleigh, to his team gave a whistle,
And away they all flew like the down of a thistle.
But I heard him exclaim, ere he drove out of sight,
**"Happy Christmas to all,
and to all a good night!"**

THE END